BIRDS OF AMERICA

BIRDS OF AMERICA

Short Fiction

Richard Rollins

Birds of America
Copyright © 2022 by Richard Rollins

All rights reserved. This book or any portion thereof may not be reproduced
or used in any manner whatsoever without the express written permission of
the publisher, except for the use of brief quotations in a book review.

Printed in the United States of America

Speedboat Books
Portland, OR

LCCN: 2022903492
ISBN: 978-1-7371412-2-8

TABLE OF CONTENTS

TABLE OF CONTENTS

TABLE OF CONTENTS

TABLE OF CONTENTS

BIRDS OF AMERICA

AMERICAN CROW
(Corvus brachyrhynchos)
Lyman, Wyoming
October 5

"I wasn't lying when I said it hurt." He put the pencil back on
the table and sat down. "You weren't fair then," he said, "and
you're not fair now." She wanted to believe him, to believe he
was right. It would be simpler that way. But he wasn't and
she couldn't. She thought of that boy in high school, Martin
or Marty, who dove head first into an empty swimming pool.
No one knew why. That was the problem with knowing, she
thought, that was where accuracy got you.

BLACK PHOEBE
(Sayornis nigricans)
Las Pintas, New Mexico
October 6

So when it was all over, she thought, grass and trees
and hills didn't mean a thing. If she had waited for him,
it wouldn't have made any difference, and if she had left,
it would have been the same. The water flowed slowly in
the irrigation ditch floating sticks, insects, and bits of dry
grass. It wasn't as if she had any choice. She had changed,
she thought, the way she felt had changed and there was
nothing she or anyone could do about it.

SAGE GROUSE
(Centrocercus urophasianus)
Wilson, Wyoming
October 6

He unlocked the tow truck winch and pulled the cable
down the rutted track to where the pickup hung with its
rear wheel over the river. And on top of that, he thought,
she said she was going to town. If she was going to town,
why did she leave the money and the grocery list on the
table. He got down on his stomach and slid the cable under
the truck chassis and hooked it. Sometimes he wondered
if there was anyone he could really trust. Sometimes he
wondered if there was anyone anyone could really trust.
There was the smell of fresh crushed sage were he lay and
below the bank the river flowed smooth and green. A fish
rose and disappeared and insects dipped onto the surface
of the water. If she was honest or dishonest, he thought,
or if she cheated or didn't cheat, it did not change who he
was it only changed the life he would live.

ROSS' GULL

(Rhodostethia rosea)
Goodnews Bay, Alaska
October 11

His brother didn't have to die, he thought. He could have saved him. He could have. He knew he could have. The wet grass lay down under his feet and the tidal mud sucked at his rubber boots. His face was twisted something terrible, he thought, from when the bullet crashed up through his chin into his skull. He dropped the gas can into the boat and swung up over the side of the gunwale. The tide was rising and running fast and the wind blew hard off the ocean into the mouth of the river. That had been a long time ago, he thought, but it never went away. It didn't matter what you called a thing. It didn't matter if you were drunk or sober or awake or asleep. It didn't matter if you believed or didn't believe. It didn't matter if you gunned the engine and pounded into the teeth of a storm hour after hour, it always found you.

SULPHUR-BELLIED FLYCATCHER

(Myiodynastes luteiventris)
Las Cruces, New Mexico
October 15

Between the shoulder of the highway and the barbwire
fence, he could see where the deer had staggered and gone
down and then, somehow, cleared the fence and gone on.
"Is there any blood?" she called. He looked back up toward
the car headlights and shook his head. He had not been
happy for a long time now, he thought, but maybe that was
not that important. He knew it would have made him feel
better to know that the deer had not been badly injured.
But maybe that was not that important. There would be
other opportunities. It was a long drive and he might come
on an accident and there would be something for him to do.

WESTERN SANDPIPER
(Ereunetes mauri)
Bodega Bay, California
October 17

"I'm not a person to be treated lightly," she said. The dog
scratched at the back door and out on the water she saw a
small boat rolling lazily near the shore. "This has cost me
a lot of time and a lot of money," she said. He kept his eyes
fixed on the patch of floor by her feet where there was a small
dent in the wood that he remembered he had made when he
had dropped the tea kettle. "Are you listening to me?" she
said. "Are you?" It would not be good to look up, he thought,
something bad would happen. If he looked up and saw her
face, he knew he would not be able to control himself and
he did not want to go down that road. He did not want to
go down a road where people suffered. He had been down
that road before. He was not going to look up and she could
think what she wanted.

CHUKAR

(Alectoris graeca)
Pendleton, Oregon
October 17

He hadn't quit on her, she would give him that. Another
car passed. Husband driving, wife in the passenger seat,
two kids in the back. They weren't about to stop. You could
squeeze a metaphor out of that, she thought. She took off
her jacket and threw it onto the front seat of the pickup
and slammed the door. Damn it was hot, she thought, or
maybe it was the hangover. She didn't deserve him but what
difference did that make. That was an old saw, like her Dad
used to say, with no teeth. Life ain't like biscuits, he used
to say, you don't just shove it in the oven. Way off down the
road she saw a big rig coming. She took off her baseball cap
and threw it into the bed of the pickup and shook out her
hair. Breath of life, she thought, and sighs of glory in the
morning.

PINK-FOOTED SHEARWATER

(Puffinus creatopus)
English Bay, British Columbia
October 20

The waitress set the drink down on the table and he cupped
his hands around the glass. Low, slanting sunlight came in
through the windows facing the bay. The bar seemed old and
tired, he thought. Too many old women, too many old men.
Old flakes off a person like dry skin, he thought, and floats
in the air and thickens it. She came into the room laughing,
almost skipping. The strands of her hair were still wet and
her eyes were bright and sparkling and full of happiness.
She slid onto the seat beside him and kissed his cheek.
I don't want to do this anymore, he thought. I don't want
to do this anymore.

GOLDEN EAGLE
(Aquila chrysaetos)
Jackpot, Nevada
October 20

He was about a mile out of town and decided that was far
enough. He pulled the car over and stopped and took the
shovel out of the trunk and climbed down into the dry wash
and started to dig. It was always about other people, he
thought, other people always trying to take what you had.
It was still cool and the early morning light was soft and
golden and the air smelled sweet. He dug the hole about
two feet deep, put the bag in it, and filled the hole back up.
The wind would scatter sand over it and in a few days it
would be impossible to find. No one will know, he thought.
No one will ever know.

BREWER'S BLACKBIRD

(Euphagus cyanocephalus)
Granger, Wyoming
October 21

"The baby is not yours," she said. He was asleep on the front seat, his head resting against the window, his lips parted, his breath slow and steady, and he did not hear her. She left the engine running and got out of the car. There were a million stars overhead, she thought, a million million stars. She walked past the headlights and down off the road into the sagebrush. It serves him right, she thought. If he had done what I wanted, it never would have happened. She stopped for a moment and listened. In the dark, beyond the barbwire fence, something moved. She unzipped her pants and pulled them down and squatted quickly. I told him the baby wasn't his, she thought. He can't say I never told him. He can't say that.

PINE SISKIN
(Spinus pinus)
Buffalo Creek, Wyoming
October 21

He pushed the horses into the corral and slid the poles
across the opening. Mist still clung to the tops of the trees
and the sound of the rapids was muffled. He would feed the
horses, he thought, and then maybe go fishing. The next
group of hunters wouldn't arrive until tomorrow. He could
go to town but he would end up getting drunk and then he
would be hungover for the long ride up to hunting camp.
He went into the tent and took off his hat and his boots and
lay down on the cot. He closed his eyes for a moment and
rubbed his forehead and then he leaned down and picked up
the book. He was reading about Alaska. That was the place
for him, he thought, when the salmon were running and the
bears and the eagles were down on the rivers. If he could
find a way to get to Alaska, he thought, he would be alright
and he could be a different man.

ARCTIC LOON

(Gavia arctica)
Aniak, Alaska
October 22

The smell of dead fish was gone now, the last hard rain had flushed the decomposing salmon off the gravel bars. He pulled up his hip boots and waded into the river. He pushed the float plane closer to the bank and clipped it into the length of rope. He was tired of explaining it, he thought. Sometimes a person simply wanted to be who they were. Nothing more than that. Nothing complicated. A movement downriver caught his eye. A bear came out of the willows about a hundred yards below the plane and moved slowly up along the bank looking into the water. Explanations were a trap, he thought, they tied you to what you said. The real truth couldn't be said because there were no words for it. That was what he'd told her, but she hadn't listened. He watched the bear stop and raise it's head. Now it sees the plane, he thought. The bear moved its head slowly from side to side and then shook it, as if trying to rid its ears of an annoying insect. It's trying to decide, he thought, and I hope for its sake it makes the right decision. He stepped up onto the plane's pontoon and opened the cabin door and slid his pistol out from under the seat.

EVENING GROSBEAK

(Hesperiphona vespertina)
Provo, Utah
October 26

"I'm not saying I'm reluctant," she said. Insects flitted over
the swimming pool and the neighbor's dog rubbed itself
along the other side of the cedar fence. "What would you do?
If you were in my position, what would you do?"
He shifted uncomfortably in the lawn chair and swirled the
ice in his drink. He wouldn't be in her position, he thought.
You don't just get dropped out of the sky someplace.
You get there by going. If you don't go, you don't arrive.
"You could tell them the truth," he said, "but to be honest,
at this point, I don't think it will save you." There were more
chairs in the backyard than there needed to be, he thought,
maybe she was planning a party. "Then what's the point?"
she said. He wanted to give her something. He wanted to
leave her something and he didn't want it to be totally false.
"The point is, you could clean the slate, scrape your plate so
to speak," he said, "and start over somewhere else."

DUSKY FLYCATCHER

(Empidonax oberholseri)
Fallon, Nevada
October 28

"I wasn't broke. Never been broke a day in my life." He
kept his hands gripped tightly around the steering wheel
and his eyes fixed on the two lane black top. She didn't care
if he'd been broke or not, he thought, that wasn't the point.
"Yes, you were," she said. "You were broke when we lived
in Prescott. You were broke and it was me that saved your
ass." Prescott was so long ago, he thought, he could hardly
remember it. That was the really truly amazing thing about
it. After all these years together, they hadn't ever lived the
same life. They had gone down the same road in the same
car, her looking out one window and him looking out the
other. Most times what she remembered they had done
and what they had said and what they had agreed to, was
so different from what he remembered, he wondered if he
had actually been there and if he had thought what he had
thought he thought and said what he had thought he said
or just imagined it.

SAGE SPARROW

(Amphispiza belli)
Rock Springs, Wyoming
October 29

"Susan won't be coming back," she said. "Not this time.
This time she's gone for good." She pulled out a chair and
sat down at the kitchen table. He picked up the can of beer
and took a long drink. It was still early, the light only just
beginning to settle below the hills. "You have friends," she
said, "people who care about you. You'll get through this.
We'll help you." They don't understand, he thought, and
probably never will. He wanted this. He chose it. He knew.
He had always known. He picked her because sacrifice was
the one thing missing from his life. He needed to sacrifice.
He needed to offer himself up. And now he had. He had
done what he had to do, he thought, and now he hoped,
prayed, he was complete.

BLACK-THROATED GRAY WARBLER

(Dendroica nigrescens)
Tuscarora, Nevada
October 29

An old Plymouth Duster sat up on cement blocks in the
yard. By the side of the house there was a refrigerator with
the door swung open. He turned off the truck engine and
sat looking out through the windshield. The front door was
closed and the shades were pulled in all the windows. There
were no animals in the yard. No dogs, no cats, no chickens
and no horses in the corral. There were four hay bales
stacked up in the open barn doorway. He reached across the
front seat and opened the glove compartment and took out
the pistol. He lay it down on the seat beside him. He didn't
like the feel of the place. He couldn't say why exactly. It
wasn't any one thing, it was a feeling. Most times when he
felt there was danger, when he shouldn't do a thing, he went
ahead and did it anyway. And most times nothing happened.
But sometimes, every once in a while, something did. The
trick was to know how to get it right. He looked at the yard
again, at the open refrigerator door and the four hay bales
stacked up in front of the open barn door and started the
engine and backed out onto the road and headed south.

CLARK'S NUTCRACKER
(Nucifraga columbiana)
McCall, Idaho
October 31

Teased out, he thought, teased out of a hole but to no good
end. The sun was warm and even though the air was cool, it
was pleasant walking. He walked along the shoulder of the
road with his thumb stuck out. He'd never been suckered
by people who couldn't find their own way, he thought.
Never been duped by the loudest and the brashest. But he'd
fallen on it this time, he thought, he'd stumbled pretty good.
There was still time to make amends but he was not going to
forget his own stupidity. He was not going to forget his own
weakness and he was sure as hell not going to forgive it.

GREAT GRAY OWL
(Strix nebulosa)
R Lazy S Ranch, Jackson Hole, Wyoming
November 1

The fire had almost gone out in the fireplace and he was asleep. She wrapped the wool blanket around her legs and leaned back in the rocking chair. She rocked slowly and the fire sputtered and popped with the last of the pine pitch. He had made it easy, she thought. There was never a day went by that she didn't think about what might have been. They might have been happy, but they weren't. They might have helped each other, but they didn't. She rocked and shadows flickered on the log walls. You never know about a person, she thought, what they can and cannot do. What they can and cannot see. You walk into a forest and you find your way out. It's not that hard. It's a bit like tying your shoes. But you never really know what a man can or cannot do.

CANADA GOOSE
(Branta canadensis)
Sauvie Island, Oregon
November 2

His son sat in his lap and held the steering wheel as they drove slowly down the grass track toward the grove of oak trees. He stopped the truck and they got out and walked under the trees toward the river. He could never have imagined this, he thought, not the walk with his small son or how he would feel. He was different now. Not because he had a son but because of the way he felt. He had never expected to feel this, had not been prepared for it. His son picked up a stick and whacked it on the ground a few times and then ran yelling down the grassy slope to the water. He was changed now, he thought, and he could never not be changed. What he knew now, he had never known before and now he could never not know it.

BROWN-HEADED COWBIRD
(Molothrus ater)
La Barge, Wyoming
November 3

"We'll pray for you," she said. "We'll keep you in our prayers." He walked out of the front yard and closed the gate and went up the rise on the gravel road and past the bull pens and the welding shed. When he reached the top of the bench, he stopped and turned around. They were still there in the front yard watching. Mary had her arm up shielding her eyes from the late afternoon sun. He wanted to remember this. Not remember exactly, he thought, but to get in down inside, down into his muscle and his bone. The white ranch house with the white picket fence, the corrals and the cattle drifting through sage brush, the bright green fields of alfalfa and the valley spreading away to the mountains. He wanted it in his blood, in the very cells of his body, so that what ever happened to him, it would be a part of what he was and when he needed it, it would be there and he could go to it.

BUFFLEHEAD
(Bucephala albeola)
Coos Bay, Oregon
November 3

"Not by me," she said, "not by me." He stepped into the living room from the patio and closed the sliding glass door. "I want you to think about this," he said, "before you do something that can't be fixed." He did not know her at all, she thought, he did not understand her in the slightest. "My friend wouldn't do that," she said. "It's as simple as that." She really can't see beyond herself, he thought, she really has no wider point of reference. "Maybe your friend is dealing with problems you don't know about," he said. She started to say something and then she stopped and pursed her lips. He could see that she was angry now. That did not go well, he thought, but then it rarely did.

WHITE-TAILED KITE

(Elanus leucurus)
Esparto, California
November 3

He backed the truck out of the driveway and the dog continued to bark on the front lawn. He drove up the street and at the stop sign, turned left down the road toward the school. There were no houses on either side now, only the grass covered lots that had never been built on. I love my wife, he thought, but it's not enough. He slowed as he neared the school and stopped. There were children in the play ground and two teachers standing and talking by the swings. She was sitting alone by the fence, her backpack on the grass beside her. Her head was back and she was looking up at the sky and he could see that she was talking. She was saying something and he knew that whatever she was saying, she was saying it in a soft, quiet, sing-song voice. I could have been a different kind of man, he thought. I could have been a better man but I'm not.

WESTERN TANAGER

(Piranga ludoviciana)
Sugar City, Idaho
November 4

Maybe when this is all over, she thought, there will be some reward. She got out of bed and pulled on her pants. He was still asleep, breathing heavily into the pillow. Her thick blond hair was tangled and matted from their sweat. She ran her fingers through it quickly and dressed and quickly went through the house and out the front door to her car. It was a beautiful cool fall morning without a hint of winter in the air. Late again, she thought. She looked at her watch. Her daughter would be waiting by the door. She would be washed and dressed and she would have made her own breakfast and packed her own lunch and her homework would be done and she would be waiting.

TREE SPARROW

(Spizella arborea)
Silver Gate, Wyoming
November 5

He hadn't been there long when it began to rain again. Later,
he thought, the moon will come out. "I wasn't following her,"
the man said. "I know it might look like I was following her,
but I wasn't. I wasn't. I swear." The man was crying. He left
the man standing on the side of the road and walked back to
his cruiser and opened the door and turned off the flashers.
He noticed the road was shiny and slick from the cold
rain. Ice, he thought. There are no graces, he thought, no
moments of extreme clarity. Not anymore anyway, if there
ever were. He knew this was not the life he was meant to
live. He knew this was not the place he was meant to be.
He knew it as sure as he had ever known anything.

DOUBLE-CRESTED CORMORANT
(Phalacrocorax auritus)
Aberdeen, Washington
November 5

"We weren't happy with the result," she said and ended
the call and turned off her phone. He turned the page of
the newspaper but did not look up. "Are you listening to
me?" she said. "I'm listening," he said. "Well, what are you
going to do about it?" He was not sure what he was going
to do about it. He knew he was not going to put down the
newspaper. Not yet. Aggression begets aggression, he
thought, violence begets violence. That was something he
had read somewhere. "I'm not happy about this," she said,
"I'm not happy at all." Someone always had to put an end to
it, he thought, someone always had to absorb it. And the one
who always put an end to it, who always absorbed it,
was the one who could.

RED CROSSBILL
(Loxia curvirostra)
Two Ocean Pass, Wyoming
November 6

I wasn't the right man for her, he thought, that's a fact.
He led the horse out of the trees and down toward the river.
The smell of snow was in the air. There was something about
her he wanted to remember, something he could always hold
on to. He remembered his lips brushing across her cheek,
her bare shoulders and the soft, smooth slope of her breasts.
But it wasn't that that he wanted to remember. A coyote
suddenly appeared in the tall grass on the opposite side of
the river. There was a small back eddy below where the
coyote stood and a cutthroat rose suddenly to take a floating
insect. Six days, he thought, six days is all I have left. In six
days I'll be home and everything will be changed forever,
everything that was will be gone.

BLUE GROUSE
(Dendragapus obscurus)
Wheatland, Wyoming
November 8

Jesus was right, she thought, right as rain. She rocked slowly
by the window. Late afternoon sunlight broke through
the low clouds and slanted into the room. She rocked and
turned the cards over one by one from the deck in her lap.
I tried, she thought, I tried hard as I could. Even if it never
happened, even if it never came about, I was right to pray.
It's the fact of the matter, she thought. It's the fact
of the matter that counts.

KILLDEER
(Charadrius vociferus)
Port Angeles, Washington
November 8

Sometimes the frustration and rejection were overwhelming, he thought, almost physical. He got up and poured himself another cup of coffee at the kitchen sink. Out on the water the ferry was disappearing into the distant rain. He could stop, he thought, he could give up. He wanted to give up. He wanted to be done with it. But he couldn't, that was the problem. Every night he went to bed determined to give up. In the morning the sun might be shining or he would hear a bird out in the pasture or a boat would be rocking gently at its mooring on the incoming tide. And he would go on. Where did that come from, he thought. He wanted to give up, why couldn't he.

PINTAIL

(Anas acuta)
Lordsburg, New Mexico
November 8

"Quick," she said. "Quick, duck down." The little girl looked at her mother and began to cry. "It's alright, Honey. Hush now, it's alright." The truck slowed and circled the front yard and drove back out through the gate. She stood up and watched it go down the dirt road, the dust trail blowing east across the fields. She looked down at her hands. They were dry and cracked and there were open cuts on her fingers. "It's alright, Honey, he's gone." There was a time when she had lain down in grass in warm sunlight and closed her eyes and drifted on the sound of insects and dreamed. How long ago was that, she thought, was it even in this lifetime.

NUTTALL'S WOODPECKER
(Dendrocopos nuttallii)
Terra Bella, California
November 10

The fire had swept through and gone up over the ridge and there was nothing left but ash and burnt trees. The moon was high and round and beautiful in the cool night air. He went up the path toward the pond calling the dog. At some point, he thought, everything has to end. At some point, everything comes undone. Here, he thought, where there once stood a ranch house and a barn and corrals and once there were horses, grass would grow again and all that too would be undone. And then he thought of the fish in the pond up ahead and imagined them surrounded by burnt trees and ash , finning lazily in the soft current that slipped past the head gate into the irrigation ditch. The cool water sparkled in the moonlight and the fish drifted over the sandy bottom, taking nymphs from the deep, rippling grass.

MAGNIFICENT FRIGATEBIRD
(Fregata magnificens)
Big Sur, California
November 11

Tree branches tossed in the wind and the rain beat down and the raccoons on the porch stared in through the glass doors but he was with her again and they were warm and together in front of the fire. They had wine and smoked salmon and they would make love again and then he would tell her and he would leave and he would never come back here again. He would go north, he thought, and he would swim naked with the seals off Angel Island one more time and then he would never go back there again. The storm rattled the cabin windows and the swaying branches knocked against the shingled roof. He loved storms, loved the untamed energy. One time up on the Chilikadrotna, on a tundra hill above the river, in a powerful storm, he lay on the wind. He let himself fall, let go completely, and let himself drop and the wind held him, held him up and rocked him.

RED-TAILED HAWK
(Buteo jamaicensis)
Owyhee, Nevada
November 11

He lay in the sage brush on the sandy rise, his rifle on the ground beside him. He could have camouflaged himself better, he thought, but he did not have the time. He needed to be back for his daughter's basketball game and besides, the horse was less than a day dead and was not putting out yet. Only coyotes had found it and a few magpies. If her team won today, he thought, they would go to state. That would be something, that would really be something. No team from school had ever gone to state. He knew. He'd played on a bunch of 'em. All he'd ever wanted in school was to go to state, to be the one, to be the first, because no team had ever gone, ever.

MOURNING DOVE
(Zenaidura macroura)
Laramie, Wyoming
November 12

He had been gone way too long, she thought, and beside she needed to go to town. It would be a surprise. Maybe they would go over to the Cowboy and have a drink. It had been a long time. She slowed the pickup and stopped at the flashing red light. She turned onto the school house road and almost hit the woman. She leaned on the horn and rolled down the window. Jesus, she was going to give that woman a piece of her mind. And then she saw them. Kids and teachers all running up the road, running as if their lives depended on it.

NORTHERN SHRIKE
(Lanius excubitor)
Lander, Wyoming
November 14

The barbwire fence ran as far as the eye could see. It ran across the sage brush flats and up onto and across the bench and up into the foothills all the way to the mountains. He backed the tractor up and set the post hole digger. The sky was a clear cool gray, he thought, like the pearl snap on a shirt and snow was coming. He had made his peace with her but it would never be a true peace. For her, he thought, the world was a place where you fought. Something was against her, something was always trying to take her down or push her down and she fought back. But the world was not like that, he thought, it did not pick or chose, it had no desire and no intent. The intent was with her and with her, there could be no lasting peace.

TOWNSEND'S WARBLER
(Dendroica townsendi)
La Push, Washington
November 15

The boat was lost but he'd lost boats before. He'd lost boats and he'd lost men. He slid a five dollar bill under the empty glass and stood up. He nodded to the bartender and went out into the soft rain. She would be working late and there was no point in going home. If she was not there, it was not home. He got into the truck and sat looking out through the windshield. He didn't know if he could do this anymore, he thought, he didn't know if he could save himself one more time. If he could, and if he did, it would be the last time. How much more did he really have in him. He backed the truck out onto the road and turned south toward the harbor. Everything was wet and glistening, he thought, the sky was low, the wind was calm and everything was wet and glistening.

BALD EAGLE
(Haliaeetus leucocephalus)
Medicine Bow, Wyoming
November 16

The big diesel cat backed slowly down the steep road, its blade up against the front of the semi-truck. The semi shuddered and bucked, its brakes trying to hold back the immense weight of the log cabin on the trailer behind it. She stood beside the cinder block foundation watching the semi, the diesel cat and the cabin inch slowly down the mud slick road. Rain poured out of the sky and beat down on the hood of her parka. The men walking beside the trailer were soaked to the skin and the mud sucked at their boots. She could already imagine herself in the cabin. It was late afternoon and the sun was shining and she was looking out of the big picture window down the mountain. She was looking down at the valley. She was looking down at the brown and the green and the long winding silver thread of the river.

SAVANNAH SPARROW

(Passerculus sandwichensis)
Arroyo Grande, California
November 17

"Eats the heart, no?" She put the gun in the glove compartment and leaned back in the passenger seat, her elbow resting on the door. "We can't go on like this," the man said. "No?" the woman said. The man looked out the window at the trailer parked in the shade of the tree. The two children sat on the steps. The girl looked steadily at the truck, never taking her eyes off the man and the woman in the front seat. She's filled with it now, he thought, there's no going back. "And the children?" he said. "What about the children?" she said. He looked at her and he tried to make his eyes seem kind. "You don't want the children to suffer," he said. "The children will suffer same as everyone, no?"

BLACK-CHINNED HUMMINGBIRD
(Archilochus alexandri)
Escondido, California
November 18

She slid the patio door open, dropped her towel on the
back of a chair, and went down the steps into the pool.
The water buoyed her up and she swam slowly, letting the
warm water slip past her cheek and over her shoulder.
What ever happens now, she thought, she had had a good
life. It had not been filled with happiness but it had been
interesting. The man came out of the house and stood at
the end of the pool watching her. He still wore his suit
and tie and she thought he still looked upset. He was a
good man, she thought, but sometimes it was not enough
to be a good man. Sometimes you needed to be capable.
Sometimes you needed to stretch out your hands and
take your life and shape it.

RING-NECKED PHEASANT
(Phasianus colchicus)
La Grange, Wyoming
November 19

He would put that all behind him, he thought, he would start
over. There was time. There was still time. He picked up
the liquor bottle from the kitchen table and poured himself
another drink. A drink and a good meal and he would start
over. He would start tomorrow. The door banged shut.
He needed to get in more wood, he thought, he needed to
buck up another cord. He needed to fix the leak in the roof.
He stood up and walked over to the door and opened it.
He sipped the drink and felt the liquor flow down his throat.
He had changed and now he could not change back. He did
not want to be who he was. He did not want to be who he
had become. He looked out at the field, at the late afternoon
light reflecting off the snow and at the brown grass poking
up through the frozen surface. Change would come, he
thought, but it would not be the change he wanted. Now, he
could never be the man he wanted to be. He could never be
the man who had never done what he had done.

BUFF-BREASTED SANDPIPER
(Tryngites subruficollis)
Oak Harbor, Washington
November 19

Despite her blessings, she thought, not because of them,
she had become a better person. Yes, in all ways a better
person, she thought. She looked down from the second
floor window to where he was working on the fence in the
backyard. If he simply did what she asked, they would be
fine, she thought, they could have a great relationship. It
seemed simple enough. But he couldn't see it or didn't want
to. She watched him pick up a cedar post and drop one end
into the freshly dug hole. He stood holding the post and
looking out across the lawn past the neighbor's house. She
followed his gaze toward the water and the boats bobbing
in the sunlight. If he loved me, she thought, he would
understand. If he loved me, he would want what I want.

WESTERN MEADOWLARK
(Sturnella neglecta)
Yuma, Arizona
November 20

It crossed her mind that this time he was gone for good, that he would not be coming back. She went out into the backyard and turned on the hose. The kids' toys were scattered all over the lawn. She filled the dog bowls with fresh water, turned off the hose and walked around to the front of the house. She locked the front door, got into the car, backed it down the driveway and headed for the interstate. It's not what you do, she thought, it's what you do when no one knows what you do. It's the difference between running and flying. It's the difference between saving yourself and saving others. It's the difference between cowardice and courage.

GREAT HORNED OWL

(Bubo virginianus)
Teton Village, Wyoming
November 21

He skied silently through the pine trees toward the river. It was the first good snowfall and elk were moving down from the high country into the valley. The air was crisp and moonlight sparkled on the snow. He skied out of the trees and up onto the dike and stopped and looked back at the mountains. He was contented now, he thought, for the first time in a long time he was contented and maybe even happy. But he knew there was something he had to do. He knew it as sure as he had ever known anything. There was something he had to do and he did not even know what it was but he knew he was not going to find it here, in this place, and he knew that when he did find it, he would no longer be contented and he would no longer be happy.

YELLOW RAIL
(Coturnicops noveboracensis)
Myers Flat, California
November 23

What would people think, she thought, what would they
really think. She had never kissed a boy, not even once.
She opened the drawer and took out the notebook and lay
it on the desk in front of her. She opened the notebook to a
blank page and picked up her pen. She looked at the clear
white page and thought of a spider. The spider was small and
black and it was in the center of a silvery web. She watched
the spider in her mind, watched it move slowly across the
web. She was not a spider, she thought, she was alone like a
spider but she was not a spider. She was timid and shy but
she was not a spider. She watched the spider raise its front
legs as if searching for something in the air. She watched the
spider for another moment and then she put the tip of her
pen to the page and began to draw.

BELTED KINGFISHER
(Megaceryle alcyon)
St. George, Utah
November 23

The car pulled off the road into the gas station and stopped
at the pump. He got up from the wooden soda box and
limped over to the car. He was still a little dizzy. The driver
lowered his window. "Fill it with regular," the driver said.
He limped to the pump, lifted the hose and flipped the
handle. His teeth hurt. He had probably broken at least one,
maybe more. But he was still pleased with himself. He had
gotten up before dawn and the painting had come easily.
A man standing with his back to the road. In front of the
man, a black twist of barb wire and a sea of gray-green-silver
sage and then mountains all bright orange and yellow. One,
two, three, just like that, he thought, the painting was done.
It was after, after that he had made the mistake.

WHITE-HEADED WOODPECKER
(Dendrocopos albolarvatus)
Entiat, Washington
November 23

She wheeled him up to the kitchen table. "You want juice?"
she asked, and looked in his eyes. His eyes said no, she
thought, his eyes said leave me alone, his eyes said go away,
his eyes said leave me in peace. She put the cup down on the
table in front of him and put the straw into the juice. "I'm
going to feed the rabbit," she said. She had already fed the
rabbit but she could not bear to watch him struggle. She
went out the back door and headed toward the shed. I'm
weak, she thought, I am so weak. What is going to become
of him. What is going to become of me. She opened the
door and went into the shed. The rabbit sat motionless in
the wire cage. She opened the cage door and scooped up
a cup of the rabbit food and poured it into the bowl. The
rabbit looked at her. "The least I can do," she said, "is do
what I said I'd do."

PLAIN TITMOUSE
(Parus inornatus)
Loco Hills, New Mexico
November 25

There were men working in the fields and she drove past them and up the road to the house and pulled into the shade. She got out and dropped the tailgate and the kids came scampering out the front door and jumped up into the truck. Maybe they didn't know, she thought, maybe they hadn't been told. She went up the steps into the house and through the living room into the kitchen. Everyone was in the backyard. They had set up four long tables and smoke from the barbecue drifted lazily into the air. She wanted to feel the right thing, she thought. She didn't want to pretend to feel it, she wanted to truly feel it and to know what it felt like. If she could feel the right feeling, she thought, feel it deep inside her and know it was true and was a part of her, then she would be the person she imagined herself to be.

LADDER-BACKED WOODPECKER
(Dendrocopos scalaris)
El Paso, Texas
November 25

He rolled up the garage door and pulled the tire cart in front of the gas pumps. He flipped the closed sign to open and unlocked the door. He had to clean the bathrooms, he thought, but that could wait. He set his coffee on the desk and sat down and opened the newspaper. Three men had been found in the desert with their hands wired behind their backs and their heads in black plastic bags beside their bodies. A pickup truck pulled into the station and stopped in front of one of the pumps and the driver got out. The driver was short and stocky with dark hair and silver bracelets on his wrists. He put down his newspaper and went out to the pump. "Fill it," the driver said. There were dark sweat stains on the driver's shirt and there was a blue tarp in the back of the truck covering something. The tarp was held down by cement blocks. He watched the driver pacing back and forth in front of the truck. He did not regret what he had done, he thought, but he had not wanted it. He thought of his wife and children and he wondered what they remembered now, when they remembered him.

YELLOW-HEADED BLACKBIRD
(Xanthocephalus xanthocephalus)
Los Banos, California
November 26

He pushed the shopping cart off the road and down under the bridge. He took the bag of food out of the cart and climbed up to where he had hidden the cardboard and the sleeping bag. He liked being under the bridge in the late afternoon because it reminded him of Paris. Everyday in the fall that year he had walked along the quay under the bridges and he remembered the dappled light reflecting off the river up onto the stone arches. He opened the bag of chips and the small can of tuna fish. He scooped the tuna out of the can with the chips and ate slowly. Sometimes he had met people who lived up under the bridges and he had wondered about them, wondered how they had come to be there. Small rocks and dirt slid past him and down the embankment. He put the chips and tuna fish back into the brown paper bag and clenched it tight. They were coming, he thought, but maybe it would not be so bad this time, maybe they would not be afraid and it would not be so bad.

WHITE-CROWNED SPARROW

(Zonotrichia leucophrys)
Libby, Montana
November 27

"Get into the car," she said. The boy stood on the lawn glaring at her, his fists clenched. "I'm not going to tell you again," she said. The boy bent down and picked up his jacket. Slowly, very slowly, he walked to the car and climbed in. She closed the door and then got into the car and put both hands on the steering wheel and stared out through the windshield at the empty plastic wading pool leaning against the side of the garage. She noticed the bird feeder was empty again. "You didn't fill the bird feeder," she said without turning around. It was a long drive, she thought, and he wouldn't be happy to see them. He would be drunk or worse and then there would be a fight and the long drive back in the dark with snow falling while the boy slept. She backed the car out of the driveway and drove past the school to the stop light. Maybe she could say the car wouldn't start, she thought, or they had a flat in the driveway or the boy got sick. The light changed and she turned left and went up the ramp onto the highway and headed north.

WHITE-TAILED HAWK
(Buteo albicaudatus)
Langtry, Texas
November 28

He walked along the sandy bottom of the dry arroyo looking
for the plants. The arroyo rose steeply on both sides but it
did not block the sunlight and it was hot. If he found the
plants here, he thought, then they probably grew in Mexico
as well and next fall it would pay to do a collecting trip even
deeper into the desert. He heard the sound of a vehicle up
on the sandy track that ran along above the arroyo. The
vehicle slowed and then stopped. He heard men talking
and then the sound of doors opening and a tailgate being
lowered. Then something heavy thudded onto the ground.
The vehicle started up and drove back along the arroyo
the way it had come. He waited until there was no sound,
nothing but the cry of a bird circling high overhead. It was
probably nothing, he thought. He found an old animal track
up out of the arroyo and climbed slowly. It was probably
nothing, he thought, it was probably nothing at all.

SURFBIRD

(Aphriza virgata)
Ocean Park, Washington
November 30

They weren't going to beat themselves up over it, she thought. "It's our responsibility," he said, "and we should do something." These things happen, she thought, what could they do about it now. "It doesn't matter what it costs," he said, "we need to fix it if we can." It wasn't going to help, she thought, to add their bodies to the pile. "I'm going to call," he said. "I'm going to see what I can do." You put your family first, she thought. Your family comes first and if you have to let others go, you let them go.

HUTTON'S VIREO
(Vireo huttoni)
Santa Ysabel, California
November 30

He sat in the folding chair in the shade. Ants had climbed
up into the empty glass and were exploring the thin residue
of beer. Flies landed on his whiskers but he did not bother to
brush them away. He tugged at the visor of his baseball cap
that had gone from white to pink in the washing machine.
His canvas sneakers had holes in the toes where he had cut
away the rubber. He could see people moving about inside
the house. The glass slider opened and a little boy ran out
squealing and jumped into the pool. The splash sent blue
waves rippling under the diving board. He did not know
how long he had been sitting there. He did not know if it had
been a few minutes or a few hours or a few days. He tried to
remember when he had sat down. He tried to find an image
in his mind of him coming out of the sliding glass door and
walking along beside the pool until he reached the chair and
sitting down. He tried to find it but he couldn't.
It wasn't there. Or if it was there, he did not know where it
was. He needed to be wrapped in something, he thought,
a sheet or a blanket. If he were wrapped in something,
he would be able to remember.

GREEN-WINGED TEAL

(Anas carolinensis)
Bonners Ferry, Idaho
December 1

People said things he didn't like. People said things that
weren't true and weren't fair but there was nothing he could
do about it now. He slid the canoe off the car roof rack and
carried it down to the river. He had stopped listening to
people. People weren't reliable. He put the canoe down on the
rocks beside the back eddy and climbed up to the car to get
the paddles and dry bag. Sometime he liked to help people.
It was okay to help people even if they weren't reliable, even if
they said things that weren't true or weren't fair. But you
had to be careful. You had to be very, very careful.

GLAUCOUS-WINGED GULL

(Larus glaucescens)
Port Townsend, Washington
December 1

The rain came in and rattled the windows and she put the tea water on to boil. He was asleep on the couch, the blanket pulled up over his shoulders. He looked pale but maybe that was just her imagination. If she thought about it, she would have to say she had been happy. But she could only say that now, looking back at what they had had. She took the tea canister down from the cupboard and opened it. He turned onto his back and moaned softly. The wind shifted around to the north and she put the tea into the pot and waited for the water to boil. Her life was behind her now, she thought, her happiness was behind her. What ever came next, it would not be that.

COMMON MURRE

(Uria aalge)
Platinum, Alaska
December 1

He should be plenty happy, he thought. They were pounding
across the bay, the throttle wide open and she was in the
bow, her long dark hair streaming out in the wind. She
was with him now and he should be plenty happy. He had
wanted her for a long time. He had wanted her ever since
he could remember. But now he was not so sure. He would
have to change and he did not want to change. They always
changed you, he thought. Women, they always changed you
or tried to. He was not good enough the way he was. He
knew that. But there was no way to be good enough, no way
to get good enough. That was all gone and it had been gone
for a long, long time, before he was even born.

BARN OWL
(Tyto alba)
Wallowa, Oregon
December 2

His grandfather and father were both gone now and he was left. He put the truck into reverse and backed it up to the the trailer. He was the one now, he thought, who had to decide the right thing to do. He hitched up the trailer and went to get the horses. She came out onto the porch with a cookie sheet of hamburger patties and put it down on the table beside the grill. She was big and round now with the baby. She picked up the bag of charcoal and poured briquettes into the grill. She squirted lighter fluid into the grill and lit it. Thin white smoke rose slowly into the cold air. He crossed the gravel drive to the corral and opened the gate. How do you know what's the right thing to do, he thought. How do you tell others the right thing to do, if you don't know the right thing to do yourself. His father and his grandfather knew. How? How did they know?

NORTHWESTERN CROW
(Corvus caurinus)
Cape Flattery, Washington
December 2

He crossed the beach to the rocks and climbed up onto the
pile of bleached logs. It was cold and the beach was deserted.
He could never find the thoughts he wanted or the thoughts
he needed when he was warm at home. He zipped up his
jacket and there was the taste of salt on the wet fog. He
needed to think now and think hard, everything depended
on it, and he needed to do something. Thoughts came into
his mind but they were not the thoughts he needed. Far
down the beach he saw a dog but he did not see the owner.
The dog was standing in the water barking at the wave break.
He needed to be able to hold his thoughts and to look at
them. He needed to be able to turn his thoughts over, like a
shell or a small stone, to examine them and find the ones he
needed. He did not hear the dog any more and looked down
the beach. The dog was in the water now beyond the wave
break and struggling. Just my luck, he thought, and jumped
down from the logs and hit the beach running.

RED-WINGED BLACKBIRD
(Agelaius phoeniceus)
Cheyenne, Wyoming
December 3

It wasn't the first time she had let things get out of control, she thought, and it wouldn't be the last. She locked the bar door and walked to her car. A light snow drifted down out of the dark sky. She had had more that one sweaty offer tonight but she needed to be home. She wanted to be home. She wanted to sit down and put her feet up and turn on the television and know that her daughter was safe and asleep in bed upstairs. Men come and go, she thought. There's always another one around the corner and who he is isn't that important anymore. She opened the car door and got in and put the key in the ignition. Light from the blue and red neon bar sign glowed through the thin layer of snow covering the windshield. It was her and her daughter now, she thought, and soon her daughter would be gone, and in the end, it would be just her.

MOUNTAIN CHICKADEE
(Parus gambeli)
Wilson, Wyoming
December 4

He dug out the snow and crawled under the log house and
began cutting the plumbing. Later, he thought, he would go
to the bar and have a few drinks before heading back to his
cabin. It was cold and wet and miserable under the house
and he was looking forward to his first drink and then he
remembered he was not going to get drunk and he was not
going to get high. He had promised himself. What good
was he ever going to be, he thought, if he couldn't keep a
promise to himself. He cut through the shower drain and
crawled on his stomach to where the kitchen plumbing came
down through the floor. The rancid smell of some kind of
animal hung in the cold air. But it was quiet and it was safe.
He needed someplace safe, someplace he was protected,
someplace he could think what he needed to think. He
watched his breath steaming out into the weak half light
coming in through the thin layer of snow that had drifted up
against the sill logs. If she were at the bar, he would drink
too much and they would go back to her place and they
would do a bunch of coke and fuck and he would have to get
up in the dark, tired and hungover, and drive back across the
river. Then he would have to put on his skis and ski to his
cabin. If it went the way it usually went, he would get two or
three hours of sleep and then get up and put on his skis and
ski back to his truck and drive to work in the dark. He did
not want that and he had promised. He had promised.

AMERICAN COOT
(Fulica americana)
Grays Harbor, Washington
December 4

If sickness was all it was, he thought, sickness would be alright. "Do you want coffee?" she asked. She put her hand over his and squeezed it gently. The waiter came and cleared the plates. It wasn't the sickness, he thought, it was the unknown and it was the fear. More than anything, it was the fear. He did not think of himself as a man to whom fear came easily. He was not even sure what it was he was afraid of but the fear was there. He looked at the people at the other tables. They were eating and drinking and talking and he felt his mind drifting. Everything was suddenly stilled and he was on a beach and the sky was gray and overcast and the wind blew the white froth off the crests of the waves and he saw the bear. It was motionless, the waves running up under its paws. It was a great brown bear, its long dark coat wet and heavy with salt spray and it was staring out at the sea.

TREE SPARROW
(Spizella arborea)
Whitefish, Montana
December 5

She turned off the television and went out onto the back
porch and opened the bag of birdseed. The feeder hung from
a snow covered branch. It was possible to do everything
right, she thought, and still not have things come out right.
It was possible to know everything you needed to know
and still not know enough. You can do all the right things,
she thought, but it's no guarantee. She looked toward the
mountains deep in snow and thought about last summer and
hiking up the ridge line. It had been hot and dry and she
had been climbing slowly and steadily for a long time. There
had been a loud crack and suddenly a huge tree had split
open and crashed onto the trail. She rolled down the top of
the bag of bird seed and clamped it with a clothespin to keep
out the moisture. She would help him one more time, she
thought, but this time, this would be the last.

ROCK DOVE
(Columba livia)
Las Vegas, Nevada
December 6

She was a dancer, she thought, and this was just one more
job in a long line of jobs. She pushed back the living room
curtains and went into the kitchen and took the toast out of
the toaster and buttered it and spread some jam. When she
was a little girl, she thought, and then stopped because she
did not want to think about it. Other people connected you
with who you had been, with what you had done, but for
her, it was like molting, like a grasshopper shedding. Past
lives were past lives. It was where she had been, not where
she was. It was hard to connect. She could remember her
past but it was hard to connect. She was a dancer now, she
thought, she was a dancer and she had a job and a house
and this was her life, this was who she appeared to be and
this was who she was.

WHITE-THROATED SWIFT
(Aeronautes saxatalis)
Blythe, California
December 6

"What about me? Did you think about me? Did you?"
He worked his way across the roof quickly, nailing the
shingles as he went. He remember her voice as if it were
yesterday. "You don't love me. You never loved me." It was
a strange thing, he thought, how people really were. How
they saw things. How they understood things. He stopped
hammering and stood up. He was tired. His back hurt and
his knees hurt but he needed to finish the job. It was strange,
he thought, how in almost everything there was a kind of
pleasure. "You don't love me. You never loved me." And it
was strange, he thought, how hard people worked to make
what they believed to be true be true.

BONAPARTE'S GULL
(Larus philadelphia)
Big Sur, California
December 6

"Even if the timing were right," she said, "I don't want to
do it until next spring." The man put his drink down and
walked over to the tall windows and looked out at the ocean.
"Are you lying to me?" he asked. She got up from the couch
and went to him and put her hands on his shoulders. "No,"
she said, "I wouldn't lie to you." He looked down at the
dark rocks and the waves and thought about how once he
had been sitting in the Anchorage airport waiting for a
flight back to Los Angeles and at the next gate people were
boarding a flight to Vladivostok. He had wondered then
what would happen if he stood and picked up his bag and
walked onto that plane. What would happen when he landed
in a country where he did not speak the language, where he
had no friends, no family, where everything was unknown
and he had to struggle every day, day after day, to live life
the way it was meant to be lived.

WHITE-BREASTED NUTHATCH
(Sitta carolinensis)
Black Rock, Utah
December 7

It was what it was, she thought, and she didn't expect more.
He had been cute and charming, in a drunken sort of way,
and she had let him fumble around for awhile before she
got down to business. The younger ones have a bit more sap
in them, she thought, but no matter how much she wanted
a man, it wasn't a cure. The sun was coming up below the
horizon and the air was crisp and clear and she thought she
could see a hundred miles, a hundred hundred miles. She
pressed her foot down hard on the accelerator and the truck
surged forward picking up speed. The air was very still and
very clear and she could see all the way to the horizon and
she could see beyond the horizon and below and she could
see what was coming.

OLDSQUAW
(Clangula hyemalis)
Pistol River, Oregon
December 8

He would've been brave, she thought, if he'd had the chance, but he never did. The nurse came in and they rolled him over and changed the sheets and the nurse adjusted the IV drip and left and it was quiet again. Somewhere out in the corridor she heard the faint pulsing of television voices. He never lied about being in the army, she thought, he only lied about what he'd done. All those years and it was the only thing he'd ever really lied about. Everybody lies, she thought. She had lied a few times herself. Everybody wants to be heroic in their own way. Everybody wants to be better than they are. Everybody wants to be bright and brave and trustworthy and intelligent. Only they're not, she thought, no one is.

PIGEON GUILLEMOT
(Cepphus columba)
Seaside, Oregon
December 9

The pity is, she thought, it didn't need to be this way. He sat in a chair on the screened porch and looked out at the rain beating down on the rising sea. She never knew what it was that had made him so angry. She never understood the threatened violence in his speech and in his eyes. She wondered if he even really knew himself why. "I'm going to go in and make tea," she said. "Would you like some?" There was a pause, as if he were making up his mind. "No," he said. "Not now." He paused for a moment. "But maybe later. Later, tea sounds good." He kept his eyes turned to the rain and the sea. He did not want tea. But he did not want to be angry because she had offered him tea and did not know that he did not want tea. And he did not want to be someone, he thought, who could not put his own wants aside.

AUDUBON'S WARBLER
(Dendroica auduboni)
Blaine, Washington
December 9

Cars were backed up at the border crossing and he let the
dog out of the truck to run on the grass. There were a couple
of college kids throwing a frisbee but the dog ignored them
and lifted its nose into the wind blowing in off the ocean.
He had meant to say goodbye, he thought, but it was easier
just to leave. They would know soon enough he was gone
when he didn't show. He had avoided the awkwardness and
any repercussions. They would not see him again soon, if
ever, and if they did, he would not be the same person and
they would probably not even recognize him. He called
the dog and the dog came running and jumped up into the
truck. He had washed himself clean, he thought. He had
swum naked with the seals off Angel Island and he had
washed himself clean. He would go north and in the north
in winter in the cold and the ice and the snow, he would
stay clean.

HORNED LARK
(Eremophila alpestris)
Lusk, Wyoming
December 9

Heaven times ten, she thought, heaven times ten times ten.
He stood bare chested in the kitchen doorway, the pistol
hanging loosely from his left hand. "Well, did you?" he
said. "No," she said, "I didn't." "You didn't, huh?" "No." He
turned and went back into the other room and she heard the
metallic pop of a beer can. The Lord , she thought, he leads
me. She got up from the kitchen table and walked slowly out
the back door and down the porch steps. She was half way
across the field, when he called her name. "Gracie!" I will
not fear, she thought, I will not fear. "Gracie, you get your
ass back here!" The Lord is my shepherd, she thought, and
started to run.

GOSHAWK
(Accipiter gentilis)
Yellow Pine, Idaho
December 10

He closed the trailer door and locked it and slid the rifle under his arm and fished through his jean pockets for his lucky nickel. He was going to need all the luck and more, he thought. The nickel wasn't in his pockets. He leaned the rifle against the side of the trailer and unlocked the door. The nickel was there on the table with his pocket knife and the half empty bottle of bourbon. It wasn't fair, he thought, and someone needed to pay. He sat down at the table and poured himself another drink. It wasn't his fault, he thought, but they blamed him anyway. He knew who's fault it was and he knew who needed to pay. He finished the drink and poured himself another and stared out the window across the field to the trees. It was the right thing, he thought, it was the right thing to do, it was the only thing to do and somebody had to do it and it was up to him. A hawk flew out of the trees into the soft afternoon light. It's rapid wing beats sent it into a long glide over the field. He could see the broad white eye stripe and the white fluffy under tail. That was the life, he thought, to come flying out of the trees in the late afternoon light, gliding effortlessly over the field, gliding and hunting effortlessly over the field. That was the life. He poured himself another drink and put his feet up on the table and unzipped his jacket. That was the life, he thought.

ROADRUNNER
(Geococcyx californianus)
Gila Bend, Arizona
December 11

He pulled off onto the shoulder of the highway, turned off the truck headlights and lay his head against the seat and closed his eyes. He had a place, he thought, where was it. Where was his place. He opened his eyes and looked at the stars and all the black dark between the tiny points of light. Somewhere there was a place for him but it was hard to find. Where? Where was it? A sudden glow lit the horizon for an instant. He opened the truck door and got out. There was another flash of light and he ran across the highway and climbed over the barbwire fence. He ran out into the sagebrush and stopped and listened. The flash of light was followed by a low rumbling. It's not safe here, he thought, it's not safe here anymore.

BROWN TOWHEE

(Pipilo fuscus)
Santa Ysabel, California
December 11

He closed the door and the singing of the congregation
faded. It was hard to do the Lord's work, he thought, it was
exacting and it was detailed. He went to his desk and sat
down. It was hard, he thought, and without more money, it
was impossible. Where would he get the money? There was
a soft tap on the door and the door opened quietly and she
came in. "We're ready for you now," she said. He sat at the
desk with his hands folded. He was tired, he thought, tired
of doing the Lord's work. "Let me help you," she said. What
was in it for him and where was he going to get the money?
She walked around the desk and helped him up. He put his
hand on her shoulder and she smelled like lilacs.

VERMILION FLYCATCHER
(Pyrocephalus rubinus)
Tombstone, Arizona
December 11

Recently she had read in the newspaper about a man in Las Cruces. His name was Johnson not Johnston, but he was short and stocky, bald and had several tattoos. The article did not identify the tattoos but she knew it was him. She looked into the mirror above the sink and turned on the hot water. All her life she had loved her long curling red hair and now it was gone. That bastard, she thought, that son-of-a-bitch. The article said the man worked at a gas station. It was him, she knew it. The article said the man had pulled a little girl out of the Rio Grande and saved her life. There was no way that son-of-a-bitch would pull anyone out of any god damn fucking river, she thought, unless there was a payday in it.

WHITE PELICAN
(Pelecanus erythrorhynchos)
Texas City, Texas
December 11

Of all the people she had ever known, parents, friends, children, he was the most trustful, she thought. More than any other person, he was the one she could trust. She brushed her hair out and looked in the mirror. She was not beautiful, she thought, not the way real beauties were beautiful, but there were those who thought she was. It was strange in a way. People looked at her smooth pale skin, her dark eyes, and her full round breasts and thought they knew something, understood something, and wanted it. But thinking you know something is not the same as knowing it. And wanting something is not the same as having it. But if he wanted this, and he did, then she would give it to him because, more than anyone she had ever known, he deserved it.

WOOD DUCK

(Aix sponsa)
Winthrop, Washington
December 11

The clear cut sloped downhill to the line of trees. He rested his rifle on the tangle of branches in the slash pile and sat down to wait. He could not see the salt block he had placed at the edge of the trees because it was the same color as the snow, but he knew it was there. He had put it there after hunting season and fresh tracks showed elk had found it. If he had had his way, he thought, she would be going back to school. He might not be the sharpest stick but he knew any school was better than no school. He looked past the stumps to the tree line and saw movement. There was something there, he thought, a light patch of brown among the evergreens and the snow and it was waiting. It was waiting for the light to drop below the hill and the shadows to lengthen and the breeze to come around. He would have sold his truck if she had wanted to go back to school. He would have found a way. But she turned him down. "It's not for me," she'd said. Who really knows, he thought, who really ever understands the consequences of what they do or don't do.

GREATER YELLOWLEGS
(Totanus melanoleucus)
New Iberia, Louisiana
December 11

He spread the blanket and smoothed it, placed the pillow against the spare tire and closed the trunk. He got into the car and started the engine and popped open another can of beer. There's a lot for folks to hate, he thought, and plenty of folks to do the hating. It was a quick run across the county line and east. No one knows what's in my heart, he thought, no one really knows. A mile before town he stopped for gas at a convenience store. He wanted to be far away from the town before he stopped again. He noticed the steering wheel was damp where his hands had been. He was afraid now, he thought, but once he started, there was no turning back. Inside the store the television was on and the girl behind the counter was filing her nails. "God, don't you just hate that," the girl said. He looked around and then looked up at the television where the girl was looking and saw a woman in bed waking up and stretching and smiling as morning sunlight slanted into the room. It was an ad for sleeping pills. "God, I just hate that," the girl said again. "I just hate it."

BLACK-LEGGED KITTIWAKE
(Rissa tridactyla)
Pacific Beach, Washington
December 12

She let the dog out onto the deck and pushed the door
closed. The dog went down the steps and nosed under the
bushes. She sat down at the small dinning room table and
looked at the pile of bills. The table was covered with bills
and letters and photos and lists of things to do. Out on
the street, a car went past and then the dog barked. It was
probably that squirrel again, she thought, and then suddenly
remembered the dream. He was sitting behind the wheel
of the blue Oldsmobile, the one they had bought with cash
off the lot in Salinas, California. He didn't look young and
he didn't look old exactly. He looked healthy and full of life.
She had never seen him look that healthy while he was alive.
He wore a short sleeved shirt with a brown and yellow flower
pattern. It was the shirt he had bought on their honeymoon
in Hawaii. He was happy. She could see that he was happy.
He was smiling and he glowed with health and happiness.
The dog pawed at the back door and she got up to let it in.
Maybe it was true, she thought. Maybe it really was true.

VIRGINIA RAIL

(Rallus limicola)
Alameda, California
December 14

He picked up the book and settled into the chair on the deck.
The sun was going down across the bay and a fresh breeze
sprang up along the beach. He sipped some wine and looked
out at the water. It wasn't his responsibility to determine
the outcome, he thought, it wasn't his responsibility to
determine it's final use. People wanted you to know more
than you knew. They wanted you to look where you didn't
want to look and to see what you didn't want to see. He put
the book down on the deck and got up and went inside. She
was watching television. If he went to her and told her it
wasn't his fault, it wasn't his responsibility, that he didn't
do anything, she would say it wasn't his fault, it wasn't his
responsibility, and besides, he hadn't really done anything.
But that was not what he wanted. It was not what he needed.
What he needed was for it to be the truth.

XANTUS' MURRELET

(Endomychura hypoleuca)
Imperial Beach, California
December 16

He stopped the truck and the boy climbed in. "Where
you headed?" he asked. "South," the boy said and turned
his head and looked out the window. Maybe they'd talk
later, he thought. Maybe they wouldn't. It wouldn't matter
much either way. It was just another long day on the
road. He always looked forward to the road and it always
disappointed. But it was better than any other place because
he didn't have to stay. Maybe later he'd show the boy the
deck of cards. Nobody can resist the pictures on those cards,
he thought. The sun was dropping slowly into the ocean and
birds were skimming over the waves. He wondered how old
she was now and if she even remembered him. He wondered
if someone was thinking about this boy. Did they miss him?
Did they want him back? Did they even care? How was it it
ended this way. His life draining through his fingers. He
needed more time. What he needed was more time.

ELEGANT TERN

(Thalasseus elegans)
Santa Barbara, California
December 17

"What?" he asked. He kept her hand in his and leaned closer. "Water," she whispered. He picked up the cup with ice water and held it and bent the straw to her lips. She sucked feebly on the straw and then turned her head away and lay back on the pillows. He put the cup back on the metal tray beside the bed. This was no struggle, he thought, no battle. This was moonlight shifting on dark water. This was a breeze that was suddenly stilled. He had come a long way to hold her hand, he thought, and every mile had been worth it. Maybe it's that what one person loses another finds. Now there was only the waiting. Waiting for the pale, silent figure at the foot of the bed to cross his legs and shift in his chair. Waiting for the pale, silent figure at the foot of the bed to straighten his tie and brush the lint from his suit. Where was the fear in that.

SPOTTED OWL
(Strix occidentalis)
Buckhorn, New Mexico
December 17

He turned off the welder and sat down with his back against the cinder block wall. He opened his lunch pail and took out the peanut butter sandwich and thermos of cranberry juice. The lunch pail was black and scratched and dented at one end. There was a spring loaded clip to hold the thermos in the lid of the pail. Every time he opened it, he thought of his farther or his grandfather because they had both carried it. Sometimes he would imagine his father in the factory yard in Buffalo, eating his lunch under a sky filled with coal smoke and dust. Their hands were the same, thick, strong, rough, oil and dirt ground into the knuckles but he ate his lunch under wide clear skies. There was snow on the mountains and coyote tracks down by the pond. You make a thing, he thought, but how do you know it's true or it's accurate. It's not the tools and it's not the desire. It can't be measured and can't be compared. You imagine a thing and you make it. You have to decide. True to what. It exists and it's real but that's not enough to make it the truth. There's always a crutch you can grab, a net you can spread, a rational or a reason. He had to decide. Had he made what he felt.

RUFOUS-SIDED TOWHEE
(Pipilo erythrophthalmus)
Moran Junction, Wyoming
December 17

He heard her yell and went out onto the porch and leaned
on the log railing and looked over at the corral. She was
standing by the gate. Her riding pants were dusty and her
leather cowgirl hat hung down her back by it's cord. "Sa va?"
he called. "Qui, c'est okay," she replied. She leaned down
and brushed the dirt off her pants and shook out her hair
and the wrangler led her horse out of the corral. "I want to
do it again," she called. "I want to do it again, right now!"
"Tomorrow," he said. "You can go again tomorrow. The
horse is tired." He suspected that it would cost him. He
didn't know it for a fact but he suspected. In Paris he had
caught her wrist just before she was about to fall. He had
pushed back the heavy drapes and found her standing on the
stone ledge outside the open window. Playing, she had said,
testing herself. Testing what, he thought. " I wasn't afraid,"
she said. "It was fun." What do you do, he thought, when
you suspect? Who do you save?

SNOWY OWL
(Nyctea scandiaca)
Oak Creek, Colorado
December 18

"Put her down here," the woman said. He put the little
girl down on the couch and went into the kitchen and got
an ice tray out of the freezer "Will she be alright?" the
woman asked. He knocked the ice cubes out of the tray
into a kitchen towel and tied the corners together. "It's just
a bump," he said, "but if she shows any signs that it's more
severe, take her to the hospital." "Thank you, so much," the
woman said. He went out and picked up his bike from the
snowbank where he'd dropped it and pedaled up the hill
through the snow to the softball field. Players from the Routt
County Doofers were already shoveling the base lines and
sweeping off home plate. How did the world go, he thought.
What were the most basic acts that drove it. Was it getting
up in the morning and tying your shoes, or was it a smile
and a handshake. If he could see what the world was really
made up out of, he thought, if he could see what lay in the
space between things, what would it look like?

LOGGERHEAD SHRIKE
(Lanius ludovicianus)
Bluff, Utah
December 18

She stepped out of the cave and shielded her eyes with her
hand against the bright sunlight. Down below she saw the
dust plume of the truck making it's way toward her along
the canyon floor. She had thirty minutes to pack up her gear
and it would be midnight before they reached the motel
and showered, had a beer and one more chicken fried steak
and hit the sack. First people, she thought, had been here
somewhere. Maybe in this canyon, in this cave, among these
rocks, maybe buried in this sand. If they were here, she
wanted to find them. She wanted to know. She wanted the
land to have a story. She wanted it to have a story she could
read and she wanted the story to tell her what had truly been
in the beginning and where it had all gone wrong.

WHISTLING SWAN
(Olor columbianus)
Brigham City, Utah
December 20

I did pray, she thought, and that prayer was not answered.
She checked the oven for what seemed like the tenth
time and went into the living room. She looked around.
Everything was ready, everything was in its place. If she
could make it through this, she thought, she could make it
through anything. She had prayed and that prayer had not
been answered and now there was no going back. People
said He had a bigger plan for him. People always said that
there was a bigger plan and not knowing was part of the
bigger plan and accepting the not knowing was part of the
bigger plan. That was extremely convenient, she thought.
Everyone knew something and everyone knew something
that no one else did. Everyone. And once you knew a thing,
you couldn't not know it. It wasn't about belief, it was about
accuracy. She knew something and she knew something that
no one else did. She knew she had prayed and that prayer
had not been answered. She knew that.

MOUNTAIN QUAIL
(Oreortyx pictus)
Lovelock, Nevada
December 20

He pushed the cattle into the corral and leaned out of his
saddle and swung the gate closed. He did not have time
to think about it now. Later, he thought, he'd think about
it. The lights were on in the machine shop. They were still
repairing the hay baler, he thought. Later, after dinner, he'd
give them a hand. Right now he wanted to wash up. He led
his horse over to the barn and dropped the reins over the
hitching rail. Did she really want another kid, he thought.
If they had another kid, he'd be stuck on this ranch forever.
He'd never be able to leave, never be able to risk it. He'd be
stuck on this ranch until he was too old to work. And then?
He had seen it before. He had seen it far too often.

LEAST SANDPIPER

(Erolia minutilla)
Nahcotta, Washington
December 20

He put the luggage on the back seat in the car and closed the door. She was still in the room and he wondered how long she would be there. He thought about taking a walk, about following the sandy path around the side of the motel and down to the bay. The tide was out and cold winter sunlight was shimmering on the wet flats and it would be pleasant to watch the birds skimming over the water or wading in the shallows. But if she came out and he was not there, there would be another round of complaints. Then there would be smoldering resentment at breakfast and barely concealed bitterness and anger on the long ride back. He had lived without her before and he could live without her again. But he was not free and he could not break free. Something held him. It wasn't love and it wasn't fear. It was something else. Whatever it was, it held him and it held him tight and he couldn't break free.

GOLDEN-CROWNED KINGLET

(Regulus satrapa)
Afton, Wyoming
December 21

He sat at the cafe counter eating steak and eggs and watched her. She was looking at herself in the cafe mirror. People passed her table coming in and stamping the snow from their boots and they passed her table zipping up their jackets on their way out. But she seldom looked away from the image of herself in the mirror. He wondered what, if anything, would break her concentration. A young cowboy came in knocking fresh snow off his coat and her eyes followed him for a moment but she did not turn her head. It would be interesting to know, he thought, what she saw there in the mirror. It would be interesting to know what she thought about what she saw. She was different, that was obvious. Different could be interesting, he thought. It could also be dangerous. He knew that from experience. He would not know which this was unless he got up and walked over to her table and sat down and asked.

BROWN CREEPER
(Certhia familiaris)
Elko, Nevada
December 21

"You bet you can't," he said and turned and walked away.
She watched him cross the lobby and go past the slot
machines and out the door. In the brief moment the door
stood open, she heard the sound of the big semi rigs idling
in the parking lot. She needed the money, she thought,
and she needed it now. There were two other drivers
seated in one of the restaurant booths and another driver
leaning against the counter waiting for the waitress to fill
his thermos with coffee. She had to have the money. She
needed the money. What she really needed, she thought,
was a boyfriend. A boyfriend with money, someone steady,
someone to give her things. And it wouldn't always be
always just about sex. It didn't always have to be always
about sex, there could be other things.

YELLOW-BELLIED SAPSUCKER
(Sphyrapicus varius)
Red Rock, Arizona
December 21

It was a common enough problem, he thought, but one he
had never expected to have to deal with. He watched the
young girls come into the store, watched them stroll up and
down the aisles looking at the clothes and cosmetics. He
followed them with his eyes, followed their long smooth
arms and the soft curling hair at the napes of their necks.
He didn't want to watch them, he thought, he didn't want to
follow them with his eyes. He wanted to be better than that.
If he really looked at himself, really looked, and saw himself
as he was, it was not a pleasant sight. But he wanted to be
honest with the man he was. He did not want to be afraid of
it and he did not want to pretend he was something he was
not. He had never done that and he did not want to start
now. But more than anything, he thought, he did not
want to be pathetic. He did not want that.

BEWICK'S WREN

(Thryomanes bewickii)
Quemado, New Mexico
December 22

He kept away from her, he thought, he kept away from
the others. It wasn't as if people wanted to know the truth.
They wanted what they thought was the truth to be the truth.
He closed the door to the shop and locked it and walked
across the packed dirt to his trailer. He went inside and took
a beer out of the refrigerator and sat down on the couch and
turned on the television. The news came on and men with
guns were firing from behind a wall in a village somewhere.
He got up and went outside and sat down on the trailer
steps. The sun was going down beyond the hills and the air
was crisp and cold. He had been a good person, he thought,
he had been raised a good person but he was not a good
person anymore and he could not find one single person who
wanted to know the truth of how that had happened,
not one, not even himself.

BLACK-FOOTED ALBATROSS

(Diomedea nigripes)
Anacapa Island, California
December 23

It was cowardice, she thought, the excuses, lies, posturing
and evasions. All cowardice. It ran through the world like
a thick black sludge. She pulled her kayak up onto the
rocks and dropped her paddle and vest into the cockpit.
Everywhere she looked, rocks and sand were splattered with
gobs of oil and birds were flapping and struggling in the
shallows. She was so angry, she thought, never in all her
life could she remember being so angry. She had called and
there would be help. She needed to get to work, she thought,
one bird at a time. There was no place in all the world that
cowardice could not reach, she thought. No matter how high
the mountain you climbed, no matter how far out to sea you
paddled, there was no place beyond the reach of cowardice.

VESPER SPARROW

(Pooecetes gramineus)
Uvalde, Texas
December 23

He backed the tractor into the shed, lowered the bucket
until it rested on the ground, and turned off the engine.
There was a fresh smell of sawdust and kerosene in the shed
and the wind whipped up the dirt and spun it around in
the open space behind the house. Two wrongs don't make
a right, he thought. He'd been taught that all his life but
he was not the kind of man to turn the other cheek. He sat
on the tractor, his hands resting on the steering wheel, and
looked out of the open shed and across the packed dirt to
the house and the fence and the fields stretching away under
the slanting sunlight. He hadn't built all this, he thought, his
father and grandfather had, but he was devoted to it.
If something happened to him, if they took him away, his
wife and his children would suffer. If he didn't do what he
wanted to do, didn't do what he needed to do, only he would
suffer. Sometimes, he thought, a man was asked to be the
strongest when he felt the weakest.

CAÑON WREN
(Catherpes mexicanus)
Salt Flat, Texas
December 25

The wind snapped the tent fabric again and then settled into a steady, hard blow. He was not crying out with pain now. She put her hands on his head, her thumbs pressed against his forehead. She wanted to draw all the pain, she wanted to do something, anything. She willed her hands to draw the pain out of him. If you've done everything you can do, she thought, and she had, you do what you can't. The wind snapped the tent again and pulled at the taut lines and he moaned. She willed all her strength into her hands and looked into her mind and waited. She saw a wide desert with blue sky and a bright yellow sun. She was there in that desert, she thought, alone and at peace. She had done what she could do and all that was left was to do what she couldn't.

CANVASBACK

(Aythya valisineria)
North Cove, Washington
December 25

He put pieces of driftwood on the fire and sat back against
the bleached log. His clothes were still damp but they were
drying. He had felt the hypothermia coming and now, with
the fire, it was leaving. He watched the waves slide up the
beach and looked at the dark line of the horizon and at the
stars. For the first time it wasn't about him anymore, he
thought. He wondered if he could live with that or how he
would live with that. Waves slid down the beach and went
away and far out to sea, he thought, carrying with them all
the possibilities and directions his life might have taken.
He stood and picked up his life vest and paddle. It wasn't
about him anymore. He was on a path and now there were
others on that path. It was about them now, about the
others, about how well he did by them.

GRAY PARTRIDGE

(Perdix perdix)
Osage, Wyoming
December 25

He pulled the hay bale off the back of the pickup, broke it open, and kicked the hay around in the snow. He broke the ice in the trough, turned the water on and let it run. Things would have been different if it had been up to him. But it wasn't and he was thankful for that. Can't say I blame her, he thought. Can't say I blame any of them. But it won't matter, not now. He pulled out the rest of the bales and spread the hay. He turned the water down to a trickle and reached into the trough and pulled out a six pack of beer. The horses were gathered at the corral fence and a light dusting of snow covered their shaggy brown backs. He was glad he hadn't seen it coming. There would have been too much time to think, to much time to decide to do the wrong thing. It was better it had come fast and unexpected, he thought, it played to his strength.

SHARP-SHINNED HAWK

(Accipiter striatus)
Eden, Wyoming
December 25

She looked out the window at the sunlight sparkling on the snow. The turkey was in the oven and they would be here soon, she thought. "I wish to god she were here," she said. He stopped peeling the potatoes and sat back. "She's happy. We can't ask more than that," he said. "I know," she said. "I know but I miss her. I miss her so much." He got up and walked over to her and put his hands on her shoulders. "I miss her too," he said. "It's not the same, now. It'll never be the same. It's what we don't know. How we'll feel. We can't ever know that." She put her arms around his neck and hugged him and turned back to the sink. Coming up the hill, up the long road, she saw three cars and a pickup truck. What she had done for so long was truly meaningful, she thought, her life was meaningful and she never had to think about it. Now, things were different, and she was not so sure.

LONG-EARED OWL
(Asio otus)
Teton Village, Wyoming
January 1

He went out of the cabin and left the door open so when
the moose came up onto the porch, it could look inside
and see he was not there. He clicked into his skis and
noticed a sage chicken had scratched through the thin layer
of snow covering the septic tank to get at the grass and that
gray-headed juncos had knocked snow off the pole fence
under the bird feeder. He skied around the cabin, past the
woodpile, and onto the frozen creek. Willow shoots and
aspen saplings, bent down by the weight of fresh snow, had
formed a tunnel. He ducked under the willows and skied
silently along the frozen creek. He saw where the moose
had been stripping willow shoots and fresh tracks showed
where elk had come down off the bench, crossed the creek,
and gone down to the river. He followed the creek until it
merged with the frozen pond. Dead whitefish had floated
up and frozen into the pond ice and coyotes and ravens had
scratched and pecked up the fish. Another good day, he
thought. They had come, the good days, one after the other,
and he did not understand how that had happened and did
not understand how that had happened to him.

WILLOW PTARMIGAN
(Lagopus lagopus)
Dillingham, Alaska
January 1

He nodded to the woman behind the ticket counter and
went and sat down in one of the hard plastic chairs facing
the runway. The small waiting room was hot and crowded
because the flight had been delayed for two days. The storm
had passed just before midnight and the crews had worked
all night and the runway was finally clear. He had taken
risks all his life, he thought, that was what he did, that was
what he was good at. He wondered if this time he had made
a mistake, if he was too old, too unprepared. When he saw
the plane taxing along the runway, he got up and went to
the window. The plane taxied to a stop and the ground crew
pushed the stairs into place by the rear door. He watched her
come down the stairs, a small yellow backpack slung over
one small shoulder, her long dark hair lifting lightly as she
descended. It's not what you know that's interesting,
he thought, it's what you don't know.

www.ingramcontent.com/pod-product-compliance
Lightning Source LLC
Chambersburg PA
CBHW021330190726

48288CB00003B/1047